DATE DUE		
DEC 2 6 '01			

Treason Stops
at
Oyster Bay

Anna Leah Sweetzer

SILVER MOON PRESS
NEW YORK

First Silver Moon Press Edition 1999
Copyright © 1999 by Anna Leah Sweetzer
Edited by Wendy Wax

For information:
Silver Moon Press
New York, NY
(800) 874-3320

Library of Congress Cataloging-in-Publication Data

Sweetzer, Anna Leah.
Treason Stops at Oyster Bay / Anna Leah Sweetzer. – 1st Silver
Moon Press ed.
p. cm. – (Mysteries in Time)
Summary: When the British seize control of Long Island in
1776, the Townsend family is forced to play host to British troops,
and teenaged Sally is torn between loyalty to the rebels
and a handsome British colonel.
ISBN 1-893110-03-6
1. New York (State)–History–Revolution, 1775-1783–
Juvenile fiction. [1. New York (State)–History–Revolution,
1775-1783–Fiction. 2. United States–History–Revolution,
1775-1783–Fiction. 3. Long Island (N.Y.)–Fiction.]
I. Title. II. Series.

PZ7.S97486Tr 1999
[Fic]- -dc21

98-52331
CIP
AC

10 9 8 7 6 5 4 3 2 1
Printed in the USA

TABLE OF CONTENTS

1

THE BRITISH TAKE LONG ISLAND

S ALLY TOWNSEND WALKED QUICKLY THROUGH the meadow toward Hannah Smith's house. She couldn't wait to tell her best friend the news she had heard that morning in her father's store. The battle in New York could begin at any moment!

George Washington and his troops had been in New York for months. The British, who'd been occupying Staten Island just south of the city, were constantly sailing their ships around New York Harbor, trying to show how powerful they were. Everyone knew there was going to be a battle. They just didn't know when. But that morning, one of her father's customers said he had heard gunfire in New York the day before.

Though the August day in 1776 was bright and sunny, Sally had too much on her mind to enjoy it. Usually she loved admiring the blue, sparkling water of Oyster Bay Harbor, which opened onto Long

Island Sound. She had spent lots of afternoons gazing toward the Connecticut shoreline directly across the Sound. But today, Sally was more aware than ever that the peacefulness of her surroundings could be very deceiving. Though she hadn't actually seen anyone preparing for battle in the town of Oyster Bay, she knew New York was less than thirty miles to the west, not even two hours away on a fast horse.

Sally knocked at her friend's front door. Waiting impatiently, she pushed back some blond tendrils that had escaped from the pile of curls pinned up at the back of her head. *What a bother—to be fifteen and too old to wear my hair loose,* she thought. But even with messy hair, Sally was considered one of the prettiest girls in the town of Oyster Bay.

After several minutes, a servant opened the door and admitted Sally into the front hallway.

"Where's Hannah?" she asked—but the servant had already rushed away. *What's all the commotion about?* she wondered, watching people with fearful expressions darting in all directions. No one paid any attention to Sally until she grabbed the arm of a woman holding an armload of blankets.

"Where's Hannah?" she demanded.

The servant yanked her arm free. "Miss Smith is in the kitchen," she called over her shoulder as she bustled up the stairs.

Sally wandered into the kitchen and found

Hannah packing dishes into a barrel. She was working quickly, stuffing hay around the dishes so they wouldn't break. Hannah was taller and stockier than petite Sally. Her light brown hair had been hastily pinned into a bun above her freckled, sunburned face. Sally noticed her friend's red and puffy eyes. When Hannah saw Sally she put down a dish and hugged her friend tightly.

"What's happening?" Sally asked. "Why are you packing?"

"Oh, Sally, didn't you hear?" said Hannah, reaching for her handkerchief. "Washington lost the battle. Long Island is now in British hands. They are heading this way right now." Hannah's eyes widened with fright. "We're all in danger—especially the Whigs." Sally knew that anyone who sided with Washington was a Whig.

"My father took part in the Provincial Congress last May," Hannah said, sniffling. "The British will know that he sided with the Rebels. They'll know he's their enemy. They'll arrest him or maybe . . . maybe do something even worse than that."

The battle was already over! Sally became frightened. Her own father took part in the Provincial Congress and supported the Declaration of Independence, which had been signed just a month ago. Everyone knew he sided with Washington. Usually Sally was able to cheer Hannah up, but she was much too upset and frightened even to try.

"What will you do?" Sally asked, shakily.

"We are fleeing to Connecticut," Hannah said. She blew her nose. "There are boats waiting down at the shore. That's why we're packing our belongings. Luckily, Connecticut is still in Washington's hands so we're going to stay with relatives there."

Sally burst into tears. "You can't leave!" she sobbed. "You're my best friend."

She remembered the day they first met, seven years ago. She had been on her way home from the market when she saw the Cooper sisters push Hannah down onto the dirt road. They were teasing her because she was big for her age. Sally remembered being surprised that Hannah didn't fight back. Even though she and Hannah hadn't been best friends at the time, Sally couldn't stand to see injustice. Though she was smaller than both of the Cooper sisters, she blurted out "If you fight with Hannah, you're going to have to fight with me too." The Cooper sisters had whispered to each other at the side of the road then turned away and went home. Ever since that day, Hannah was devoted to Sally. And Sally grew to love Hannah like one of her own sisters.

"*Your* family should go too," Hannah whispered. "Who knows what will happen when the British get here."

"Maybe the war won't last long and you'll be back soon," Sally said, hopefully.

Just then, Hannah's mother entered the kitchen. She, too, had been crying. She held a small handkerchief to her nose. "Sally, please tell your dear mother I am sorry I didn't have time to say goodbye. I will think of her and pray for your family every day we are gone." She gave Sally a quick hug and then turned to her daughter. "Hannah, the boats are ready. It's time to go."

"But Mama, I'm not done packing yet," Hannah cried.

"There's no time to finish," her mother said gently. "We will have to leave some things behind." She left the room.

Hannah put her arms around Sally. "I'll pray for you every day," she promised.

"I'll miss you so much," Sally said. "I'll be watching the harbor every day, waiting for your boat to return."

The two girls walked out the back door, arm in arm. Sally was crying so hard she barely managed to say goodbye. She watched as her friend walked with her mother, father, brothers, and all their servants toward the harbor where the boats waited. Hannah turned around one last time and Sally waved. Then she watched as they boarded the boats, got settled, and pushed off from shore.

Suddenly, Sally remembered her own family and her stomach tightened with fear. She wondered if her mother and father knew that the British had control of Long Island. She hurried home to warn them. The closer she got, the more worried she became, running the last several yards up Main Street.

Finally she reached the Townsend family home. When she had left, her father had been sitting on the porch of their fine, two-storied house. Now the large porch that stretched across the full length of the house was empty.

Sally burst through the front door, went into the parlor, and gasped at what she saw.

2

THE ARREST

SALLY WAS HORRIFIED TO FIND TWO LARGE soldiers, wearing red coats and white breeches, roughly holding her father by his arms. Another soldier stood close by, watching. Sally knew he was a captain because of the gold braid on the shoulders of his coat and the red sash tied around his waist. Mr. Townsend's hands were tied behind his back. Sally's father was a well-to-do store owner and very well respected in Oyster Bay. *How could anyone dare to handle him like this?* Sally wondered with horror.

"No, Papa!" she cried. "They can't take you away." Her knees shook uncontrollably until finally she sank to the floor.

"Shut up, girl . . . or else . . ." the British captain threatened sharply.

"It will be all right, Sally," Mr. Townsend said. "I'll be home soon."

"Hmph," the officer sneered. "You *think* you will be home soon."

Sally's mother rushed down the stairs, holding a large bag. Sally stood up shakily, ran to her mother and put her arms around her mother's waist. She was too afraid to ask what was happening.

Mrs. Townsend pulled Sally's arms away. "Quick, Sally," she said in a hushed tone. "I need you to gather some things for your father. We only have a few minutes. They're out saddling a horse for him. Phebe is upstairs packing some clothes and blankets. Go to the kitchen and help Audrey. Fill a sack with bread, fruit, vegetables, and whatever cakes or cooked goods are there." Then, in a whisper, she said, "I don't think he'll be fed very well on a prison ship."

When Sally heard the words *prison ship* she hurried into the kitchen in tears. She didn't want her father or the soldiers to see her crying.

The kitchen was behind the dining room, which Mr. Townsend also used as his store during the day. The parlor was across from the dining room, and there was a bedroom behind it. Sally could hear Phebe moving around in her parents' bedroom above, one of four large rooms upstairs.

Audrey was busy opening and closing cupboards, gathering all the food she could find. Together the two girls filled a large sack with as much food as it could hold. Then, together, they returned to the parlor. Mrs. Townsend and Phebe were already there, sobbing as they handed Mr. Townsend's things over to the soldiers.

Before leaving, the British captain walked over to the wall where a portrait of a young sea captain hung.

"Who is this?" he demanded, looking at each of the Townsends.

Nobody said a word.

"I said, who *is* it?" the captain yelled, stepping toward Audrey and Sally.

"That's . . . my oldest boy, Solomon," Mrs. Townsend stammered. "He's away on his ship." "Too bad," said the captain, seeming satisfied with her answer. "We could have had *two* prisoners today."

Solomon, Sally's oldest brother, was the captain of a relative's merchant ship. *Thank God his ship is far away in Europe,* Sally thought. Then another wave of fear passed through her body as she remembered her other brothers.

Early that morning, two of them, William and David, had taken a boat out on the Sound to fish. They often fished for the family and probably wouldn't be home until dark. Sally was glad they weren't here to see their father's arrest. But where was Robert? Sally prayed that Robert wouldn't walk through the front door any time soon. Her tall, confident brother, who had a great sense of humor, was twenty-two years old and worked with their father in the store. The British would certainly arrest him if he were here.

At least the British soldiers had no interest in taking the Townsend women away. But Sally didn't like the way they were staring at her and her two older sisters. She was used to people looking at them when they walked through town—they were all pretty and petite with curly blond hair. Usually Sally would smile at an admirer. After all, she didn't want them to think she was too proud. But she didn't smile at the soldiers.

Audrey and Phebe weren't smiling either. Twenty-year-old Audrey was very composed, though she hardly ever showed her feelings even under normal circumstances. She was practical, hard-working, and smart. Seventeen-year-old Phebe was equally smart and hard-working, but she was also very emotional. Now she was clinging to her mother, sobbing quietly.

Sally's thoughts returned to the scene in front of her. The captain was looking around the room. When he spotted Mr. Townsend's musket above the fireplace, he pulled it down. Then he turned to face the others. Sally felt her heart pounding. She could hardly breathe. Was he going to start shooting? Was he going to shoot Papa right there in the parlor?

"God, no. Please, no!" Phebe screamed between sobs.

The captain, wearing a nasty, crooked smile, came so close to Samuel Townsend that their faces were just inches apart. Without even flinching, Mr. Townsend returned the officer's stare.

Sally was proud of her father. He was the picture of dignity, standing tall, wearing plain, finely tailored clothes. His hair was tied back neatly behind his neck.

"Do you think I would leave the enemy with a weapon?" the captain asked. He lifted the musket above his head and slammed it hard against a small wooden table. He slammed it down again and again until both the gun and the table lay on the floor in pieces.

"Let's go," the captain barked to the soldiers.

Mrs. Townsend put her arms around her daughters' shoulders as they helplessly watched their father. Mr. Townsend was speechless. He looked sadly into his wife's eyes as he passed.

"Samuel!" Mrs. Townsend whispered.

The captain was the last to leave. "You have some attractive daughters, Mrs. Townsend," he said, with a crooked smile. "I'll be sure to come back to call on them." He tipped his hat to Phebe, who turned her tear-stained face away. He left without another word.

Suddenly, the house was quiet. As Mrs. Townsend and her daughters stood with their arms around each other, the only sounds in the room were sniffles and sobs.

WILLIAM AND DAVID RETURNED HOME just as it was growing dark. They rushed through the back door, quickly laying their string of fish aside, and found their mother and sisters in the parlor.

William's eyes were shining with excitement. "The soldiers are everywhere," he said.

"They're setting up camp in people's yards," David said.

"And staying in people's houses without even asking," William added.

"As soon as the Smiths left, the soldiers moved into their house. We saw them. We . . . what happened?" The two brothers had been so caught up in their excitement, they hadn't noticed the four tear-stained faces until now. Even Audrey had finally broken down and cried.

"Boys, they have taken your father," Mrs. Townsend said.

The excitement drained from their faces as William and David stared at their mother.

"They took him away," she repeated, dabbing at her eyes with her handkerchief. "We must do something."

"About what?" asked Robert, stepping into the parlor.

Sally looked fondly at her older brother. Robert was quite heavy, though Sally preferred to think of him as well fed. He had dark hair and warm, brown eyes. Though Robert was seven years older than Sally, they were closer to each other than they were to their other siblings. They understood each other and had many similarities. They were curious; they enjoyed long walks along the Sound, and they loved a good joke. Whenever Sally was in low spirits, she could always count on Robert to cheer her up. And Robert counted on Sally in the same way.

"British soldiers came and took Papa," Audrey said quietly. Phebe burst into fresh sobs.

"When? Where?" asked Robert, shocked.

"A few hours ago," said Audrey. "They took him to a prison ship."

"I think they took him to Jericho first," said Mrs. Townsend, trying her best to remain calm. "At least *you're* home safely."

"We have to find a way to get Papa back," Sally said.

"There must be a way . . ." said Robert, trying to think of a plan. Sally had never seen her brother look so serious. They all sat in silence, praying for an answer to come to them.

"It's so hot in here," said Phebe. "It's sweltering."

13

"William, will you get your sister a glass of water, please," Mrs. Townsend asked.

"I'll get it," said Audrey, heading toward the kitchen. "All this commotion must be too much for Phebe."

Sally's eyes met Robert's in a knowing glance. They had been through many of Phebe's fainting spells before. Sally remembered the time Robert had said he was glad she wasn't delicate like Phebe. She was strong and feisty like him, and was always up for a dare—swimming in October, jumping off the barn roof, or crawling into the cellar among hundreds of spider webs. But at the moment, she wasn't feeling very brave at all.

"I think I've got it," Robert exclaimed. The others looked at him hopefully, as Audrey came back into the room with water for Phebe.

"We have money from the store," Robert continued "which means, we can ransom Papa back."

"How?" said Sally, admiring her brother's brilliance before she even understood the plan.

"If Mama pays the soldiers with the money from the strong box, they'll let Papa go," Robert explained. The strong box was where Mr. Townsend kept the earnings from the store.

"What an excellent idea," said Mrs. Townsend, dabbing at her eyes with a handkerchief. The others agreed, optimistically.

"We must get him back before they lock him up on a prison ship," Robert said. "He could easily die on one of those terrible ships."

Sally jumped up from her chair. "I'd like to get every single one of those soldiers back," she said. "I hope *they* all die."

"My lively little Sally," Mrs. Townsend sighed. "You have such strong beliefs—but we don't think like that."

"I know, I know," Sally said, rolling her eyes. She began to recite: "Quakers do not believe in violence or revenge. Quakers do not take sides either. We must remain neutral, in the middle, no matter what happens." Sally sat down again, frustrated.

"Mama," Robert said gently, "Sally can't help the way she feels. And I don't know how we can keep from taking sides after this."

"Still," Mrs. Townsend insisted, "it's more important than ever to try to hold fast to our principles." She went to get her hat.

"Mama, you *can't* go," said Robert. "It's nearly dark. A woman shouldn't be out at night making deals with soldiers."

"Especially the horrible ones that were here today," Sally added.

"I'll go, Mama," said Robert, putting a hand on her shoulder.

"No, Robert," Mrs. Townsend said thoughtfully.

You could be arrested too. I don't know what to expect from these men, but I am sure they wouldn't hurt a woman."

Everyone was silent, hoping she was right. Sally looked at her strong, fearless mother with admiration.

"I'll take Audrey," Mrs. Townsend said. Phebe's too nervous and Sally, you're likely to lose your head and get us into more trouble. Audrey is calm and sensible."

Sally smiled at the truth in her mother's logic though she wished she could be the one to go. Before long, Mrs. Townsend and Audrey set off on their horses toward Jericho, with all the money they had.

Sally said a silent prayer for her brave mother and sister as she watched them ride down Main Street.

Mama and Audrey seem so defenseless, she thought, *especially for such a dangerous mission.* British soldiers and common thieves lurked everywhere.

She glanced at Robert, who sat silently, his shoulders slumped as he stared at the floor. She knew that he wished he had gone instead of their mother and Audrey, but it was clear that this was the best plan. They just had to wait.

3

HOUSEGUESTS

MRS. TOWNSEND AND AUDREY HAD BEEN gone for hours, and it was getting harder and harder for Sally to ignore the horrible possibilities. Phebe, William and David had gone to bed, but Sally and Robert sat in the parlor waiting.

"Jericho is only five miles away," said Sally. "What's taking them so long?"

Robert shrugged with frustration. This was the first time she could remember that they weren't able to cheer each other up. She knew Robert must be filled with the same thoughts as she. *Where were Mama and Audrey? Did they have to go further than Jericho? What if they were too late and Papa was already on a prison ship?*

Suddenly, the front door flung open. Sally and Robert jumped to their feet as Mr. Buchanan, entered the parlor.

Sally was surprised to see Mr. Buchanan, who

was married to her cousin. Mr. Buchanan was a large, robust, jolly man, always ready to help the Townsends when it was needed. In fact, he had helped Solomon invest in a merchant ship for him to captain.

Audrey and Mr. and Mrs. Townsend followed him. "Papa!" cried Sally, running over and giving her father a big hug. Sally noticed he was showing the effects from his ordeal, with tired eyes and sagging shoulders.

Mrs. Townsend smiled as she clung to her husband's hand. "Audrey suggested we ask Mr. Buchanan to help us," she said. "We're lucky he was able to help us bargain with those awful soldiers."

"Did the money help?" Robert asked.

"Several thousand pounds helped very much," Mr. Buchanan said, grinning.

Sally gasped. "That's a fortune!"

"It was a small price to pay to keep me away from a prison ship," Mr. Townsend said. "Everything is all right now."

"You look exhausted, Papa," said Robert.

"We're all exhausted," said Mrs. Townsend. "Let's all say good night to Mr. Buchanan, and then go to sleep."

A FEW DAYS LATER SALLY REALIZED that even though Papa was home, everything was *not* all right.

The same British captain who had arrested him came back again. One of the Townsend's slaves led him into the parlor where Mr. Townsend was working over his ledgers. Sally was upstairs when she heard his loud, familiar voice. She went to the stairway, in the center of the house, and sat on the top step. From there she could hear everything being said in the parlor—she could even see a small section of the room.

"So you are back again," the captain was saying with a sneer. "I hope your little trip was enjoyable."

"Please leave my house," Mr. Townsend said. If he was feeling any anger, he did not show it.

The captain sat down on an overstuffed chair and leaned comfortably to one side. Sally fumed as she watched him toy with a lace doily on the table next to him. "Mr. Townsend, you don't seem to understand," he said sharply. "I can go wherever I wish. Today I wish to be in your parlor."

"What do you want from me?" Mr. Townsend asked calmly.

The captain gazed around the room. "You have a fine house here—the biggest in Oyster Bay, in fact. I have some men who require a place to stay. I'd like them to stay here and I'd like you to make every comfort available to them."

"That would be impossible," said Mr. Townsend. "This is a large house, but we have no spare room."

The captain leaned forward. "I want you to *make*

room." He stared intently into Mr. Townsend's eyes with hatred. "There will be eight or more men here this afternoon. Make sure they feel welcome. I don't want to hear any complaints from them about your hospitality." He stood up, walked out of the room, and slammed the door behind him.

Sally wanted to go to her father, but she didn't want him to know she'd been eavesdropping. Instead, she went to her room to be alone. *Where would everybody sleep? Did they expect the Townsend women to cook for them? When would this horrible war end?*

Sally, along with her mother, Phebe, and Audrey, worked hard to prepare rooms for the soldiers. The slaves who worked in the house spent hours washing the linens for their uninvited guests, and preparing larger amounts of soup, potatoes, bread, and cake for their supper. William and David moved their belongings into Robert's room, while Sally helped Audrey and Phebe move their possessions into her room. Mr. and Mrs. Townsend would stay in their chambers. That left one large bedroom upstairs and one downstairs for the soldiers' use.

By the time the soldiers arrived that afternoon, the Townsend women were exhausted. They tried as hard as they could to be polite to them. But within the first few minutes the family realized how difficult it would be to be civil and kind to the soldiers.

Mr. Townsend tried to guide them to their rooms, but the men wandered noisily throughout the house, rudely examining their surroundings. Sally heard one soldier rummaging around in the kitchen, probably looking for something to eat. Mrs. Townsend seemed to be in shock as she stood in the center hall, staring at the mud the soldiers tracked in on her finely polished floor.

Sally watched as on of them picked up her embroidery sampler in the parlor, laughed and showed it to another soldier. A sampler was a piece of cloth that a young lady used to show off how well she sewed, using different patterns and stitches. Sally felt her face flush with anger and embarrassment. Sewing was an endless chore and she was never very good at it. *These men have no manners,* she thought.

That evening, before they ate their own meal in the kitchen, Sally and Phebe served supper to the soldiers in the dining room.

"They eat like pigs," Sally commented to Phebe in the kitchen.

"We shouldn't say bad things about them," Phebe said piously. Then she lowered her voice and said "But they *are* pigs. I dread having to clean their rooms every morning." It had been decided that Phebe, Sally, and Audrey would clean the soldiers rooms and serve them supper while the slaves took care of their other needs, such as bringing pitchers of water to their rooms and helping prepare the huge quantities of food they greedily consumed.

"So do I," Sally said. "They have absolutely no regard for us."

Just then a soldier called, "Girl, girl, bring me more."

"See, they act like we're *their* servants," Sally said, gritting her teeth.

"Please, girls," Mrs. Townsend said, entering the kitchen. "We must try to be tolerant. Up until now, there have only been love and good feelings in our home. I would like that to continue."

Sally picked up a platter of bread and potatoes. "It's not going to be easy," she muttered, heading into the dining room.

IT DIDN'T TAKE LONG FOR SALLY to find that Phebe had guessed right. The soldiers kept very messy rooms. She knew that if the rooms weren't cleaned every day, then they would smell. She wondered if the soldiers ever washed.

One morning after the soldiers had been there a week, Sally sat on the front porch mending. She was trying to hurry through a pile of William and David's shirts, stockings, and linen breeches. Now that she had more chores than usual, she had to rush through them in order to have any time to herself. Sighing, she thought about how quickly her brothers tore holes in the knees of their breeches. It was a good thing the Townsends owned fields behind their house where they grew their own flax. Even though Mr. Townsend owned a general store, it was wartime and already it was hard for him to keep his business stocked with necessities.

The Townsend home was situated on bustling Main Street, with the fields, orchard, sheds, and smokehouse behind the house, extending to Oyster Bay Harbor. Although Sally enjoyed sitting on the front porch so she could see everyone who passed on the busy street, today she was trying to hurry, and didn't pay attention to the horses and carts passing by. But when she heard the sound of horse hooves stop in front of the house, she looked up.

"Robert!" she cried, dropping her mending and walking to the gate to greet her brother.

Robert had just come back from New York. He usually made the trip once a week to buy goods to resell at the family store. Robert smiled as he dismounted. "My dear little sister, always working," he said. "Don't you ever have any fun, Sally?"

"You know what they say," Sally said grinning. "Trouble comes to those who are idle. It's good to have you home. It's not as much fun when you're not here. Not that I have time for any fun these days."

"I brought you a present from New York," Robert

said, handing his sister a package.

"But Robert, you didn't have to buy me anything," said Sally. "With everything so scarce, I'm sure you paid too much."

"No price is too high for my favorite sister," Robert said and winked.

He watched eagerly as Sally tore open the package. She held up a soft, gray, wool shawl. "Oh, how beautiful," she exclaimed, holding it in front of her. "You shouldn't have." She was very pleased. "I hope you got one for Mama, too."

"Of course I did," said Robert. He put his arms around her waist and twirled her around.

"Let me go!" Sally squealed. "Oh, you're so silly." She giggled as he continued to spin. "Please let me go!" She glimpsed their neighbor Mrs. Hawkins, watching them from across the street as she swept her porch. It seemed as if she was always sweeping. "You're making a scene," she hissed into Robert's ear.

"Hello, Mrs. Hawkins." Robert called. "It's a fine day for dancing, isn't it?"

Mrs. Hawkins shook her head with disapproval, but couldn't help smiling a little.

"I'd like to play a trick on her," Robert whispered mischievously. He let Sally go.

"Like what?" Sally asked, catching her breath.

"She always leaves that broom out on the

porch," Robert said. "When she goes inside we can loosen the binding. Then when she goes to sweep again, all the straw will fall out."

"Robert, that's so cruel," Sally giggled.

"You're right," he said. "Instead, I'll tell you a joke I heard today."

"I'm listening," said Sally, leaning on the gate.

"A man passed by a Redcoat riding a horse. He said, 'Sir, that's certainly a nice pig you have there.' The Redcoat yelled, 'This is not a pig. It's a horse.' The man said, 'I was talking to the horse!'"

Sally watched her brother laugh heartily at his own joke. "That's not nice, Robert."

"I know," Robert said. "And I guess they can't help what they look like. And speaking of Redcoats, just as I got into town, I saw two of them ordering Old Man Goodwin around. They said, 'We want your hay! Turn over your cartload of hay.' You know how Old Man Goodwin is."

Sally nodded. Mr. Goodwin seemed to think more slowly than other people and usually kept to himself.

"He just sat up on that cart and didn't move—even when they stuck their guns in his face. Finally, Old Man Goodwin got off the cart and pushed it over, spilling the hay into a big pile in the middle of the street. Then he rode away in his empty cart, leaving the Redcoats looking at the pile of hay."

"Do you get it?" Robert asked. "They wanted him to turn his cart over to them, but he really *turned* it over. Hah ha. That showed them!"

Sally laughed. Now that Hannah was gone, she appreciated Robert more than ever.

Robert took his sister's arm. "Let's go down to the harbor to see if William and David are on their dinnerbreak yet," he said. " I want to see if the fish are biting."

As they walked along the shoreline, Sally tried to forget about her unfinished chores. "Robert, it's terrible what the British are doing around Oyster Bay," she said. "They're so rude to us and just take whatever they want."

"I know," he replied. "Even people who thought of themselves as Tories are beginning to change their minds and side with Washington."

"And there's nothing we can do," said Sally, sighing.

"Listen to what I heard in the city," said Robert. "A Patriot was hanged for passing information to Washington's men. Nathan Hale was his name. He was giving them information about where the British troops were and how their supplies were holding out."

"How awful," Sally said. "I get the feeling the British would imprison any of us—even if they only *suspected* us of conspiring against them."

"You're right," Robert said. "We all must be very careful to appear as if we are not taking sides. You know how I feel, though."

"I know," said Sally. "They forced Papa to sign and carry around a piece of paper that pledges his allegiance to King George III. He doesn't mean it though. He doesn't feel it in his heart.

Robert pulled a folded piece of paper out of his coat pocket and handed it to Sally.

She read:

This is to certify that Robert Townsend

hath submitted to government and taken

the oath of allegiance to his Majesty King George

this 10th Sept. 1776 before me.

Whitehead Hicks, Supreme Court Judge

"I have to carry around the same kind of paper as Father, even though I'd like to burn it," said Robert. "We must be careful. If it appears as though we are helping the rebel side, it could mean death."

This puzzled Sally. Though she didn't like the British, she certainly wasn't going to help the Rebels. She had no interest in actively helping either side.

They walked past Hannah's house. The yard used to be well kept with pretty flowers surrounding the whitewashed little home. Now the yard was littered with garbage and discarded equipment from the soldiers who were living there.

"You must really miss Hannah," Robert said quietly.

"I do," Sally said sadly. "But I *am* glad she doesn't have to serve any Redcoats." The thought of her best friend made her heart ache.

Just then, they reached the harbor. William and David had arrived back at shore only minutes before with a bucket full of fish. They would still need another bucketful, though, to feed all of their rude, hungry guests.

4

TAKING SIDES

ONE AFTERNOON SALLY AND PHEBE WERE walking home from a neighbor's house. Since the British occupation, Mr. and Mrs. Townsend insisted their daughters never go anywhere alone. The Redcoats, who were camped around the town, made them nervous. They made Sally nervous too. She never knew what they were going to do.

As the two sisters walked along, they had to pass a British campsite, an open field that had been cleared except for a few shade trees. Several months earlier, a neighbor of theirs had planned to build a house on the land but, because of the war, the plan had been postponed. Now, a group of about thirty soldiers had set up camp there.

Sally hoped the soldiers wouldn't stare at them but, just in case, she gripped Phebe's arm. "Don't look like you're afraid of them," she said. "If they think we're afraid, they might do something."

"Look at the way they live," Phebe said. "Like animals." It was true. The field around the tents was littered with garbage. Since there were no separate stables for their horses, there was a strong, barn-like stink.

"Don't even look at them," Sally whispered as they passed.

"Hello ladies, it's a fine afternoon, isn't it?" yelled a deep voice. Out of the corner of her eye, Sally could see that the voice belonged to a soldier sitting on a log and shining his boots.

"Would you like to sit with us for a while?" called another soldier who was eating an apple.

"Keep walking," Sally hissed without moving her lips. She gripped her sister's arm tightly. "Don't look. Don't turn around."

As they followed a bend in the road, they could hear the soldiers laughing.

"You're hurting my arm," Phebe complained.

"Sorry, I didn't realize it," Sally said, relaxing her grip. "Look, there are two more up ahead. Don't they ever have anything to do?"

"No," Phebe replied. "They have nothing to do because the town provides them with everything they need."

They quickened their pace, silently trying to pass the two soldiers.

"Here are some pretty young ladies to keep us

company this afternoon," said the taller soldier.

"The prettiest we've seen all day," said the shorter one.

Ignoring them, Sally and Phebe continued walking—until the shorter one grabbed Sally's arm.

"Let go of me!" she cried, trying to free herself. But the soldier's grip was firm. Sally's heart pounded with fright. She had never been this close to a strange man before. Phebe held tightly to Sally's other arm, terrified.

"How about a little kiss?" said the shorter soldier.

Sally's heart pounded even harder. She was used to soldiers making rude comments, but this was the first time any of them wanted to hurt her. Knowing she had to take action, she kicked the shorter soldier and gave her arm one last yank. She heard a tearing sound but could not take the time to figure out what it was. Nor did she have time to pick up the basket she had dropped as she broke free. Hand in hand, she and Phebe ran away as fast as they could. Phebe tripped on her long skirt and nearly fell, but Sally pulled her up and let her regain her balance. They heard the soldiers laughing loudly behind them until they were a few houses away from home.

Breathlessly, they let themselves in and hurried into the parlor where Mr. and Mrs. Townsend and Robert sat talking. Phebe fell into Mrs. Townsend's arms, sobbing while Sally caught her breath and told her family members what had happened.

"What kind of people are they?" Mr. Townsend said furiously. "Attacking women?"

Sally noticed that the edge of her sleeve was torn and realized that must have been the tearing sound she had heard. She saw Robert notice it too as he sat in angry silence.

"They ripped your clothes?" Mr. Townsend asked, also noticing the tear. Sally nodded. "They *touched* you?" he roared.

"And she dropped her basket when she kicked him," Phebe said, sniffling.

"That's it! I've had enough!" Robert yelled, jumping up and storming up the stairs to his room. The rest of the family watched him go in silence.

He came down, about a half hour later, while Sally and Phebe, still upset, were telling Audrey what had happened. When Sally saw Robert, she stopped talking for a moment.

"Robert, what is going on?" she asked. "Your clothes . . . they're so fancy." He wore ruffles at his neck and at his wrists and, instead of his usual gray coat, he wore a deep, rich purple coat. "I don't understand . . ." she continued. *Why was Robert acting so odd?* She wondered. Quakers usually dressed in plain clothes.

"I bought these clothes a few weeks ago because I had an offer," Robert replied, pausing mysteriously. It was clear he didn't want to tell his family too much. "I haven't put them on because I didn't know if I was going to accept the position until now."

"What kind of offer, son?" Mr. Townsend asked, looking puzzled.

"A man named Mr. Rivington presented me with an offer of a partnership," Robert answered. "He wants to open a coffee shop in New York. With all the soldiers quartered there, it would make a fortune." He paused before speaking again. "Rivington also owns a newspaper—*The Royal Gazette*. He asked me to write some articles for it. Of course, he wants news about New York—not Oyster Bay."

"Would you have to live in the city?" Mr. Townsend asked.

Robert nodded.

"What?" Mrs. Townsend asked, unable to believe her ears.

"But you can't leave . . ." Sally exclaimed. How could he be talking about going away to make money when his family needed him?

As if her father could read her mind, he said, "How can you think of leaving, son. We need you here." Everyone nodded in agreement.

"That is why I am leaving," Robert said. "I must do something to help."

Sally watched Robert call for his horse to be saddled. *How could he help by going away?* she wondered, following him out to the street.

"You should be inside, Sally," Robert said, gently.

"Robert, I don't understand why you're doing this. You've always told me everything. Why can't you explain how this will help us?"

"Please trust me, Sally," Robert said, putting his arms around her. "I just can't tell you about this." Then, in a brighter tone he said, "You act as if New York is at the other end of the world. It's only thirty miles away." He mounted his horse as Sally's eyes filled with tears.

"I'll be home every week, I promise," he called as his horse began prancing down the street.

Sally watched him ride away, confused by her brother's strange behavior.

AS HE HAD PROMISED, ROBERT FELL into a pattern of paying weekly visits back home. He always brought the Townsends reports of the war. It seemed as if General Washington were losing. His army had very little money for supplies, and morale among his troops was said to be very low.

During these visits, Robert spent the most time with Sally. "General Clinton has dug in and built fortifications in Manhattan," he explained to her one day. "Washington is watching him closely, waiting for him to move out of the city so he can attack him. Neither one of them wants to have a battle there. If that were to happen it would be a major confrontation, and neither of them wants to risk losing a large part of his army."

Robert noticed Sally's pained expression. "What's wrong?" he asked.

"This war has been going on for too long and I'm sick of it," Sally said with disgust. "Something *has* to happen soon."

5

THE QUEEN'S RANGERS

SALLY HAD TO WAIT A LONG TIME FOR THINGS to change. Days became weeks and weeks became months.

It was a cold, fall morning in 1778, two long years since the British soldiers had moved in with the Townsends. Sally looked in her bedroom mirror and frowned, thinking about how happy and innocent she had been before the British took Long Island. Now, she felt weary and much older than her seventeen years.

Even though she'd been attending the peaceful Quaker meetings with her family, she couldn't help detesting the British. They appeared to have no feelings of love or compassion. All they seemed to know was cruelty.

As Sally studied herself in the mirror, she heard the sound of horse hooves and marching. Out her window she saw hundreds of British soldiers either marching or riding into town.

Later that morning, she heard from a neighbor that British Colonel John Graves Simcoe had arrived in Oyster Bay. He had decided it was the perfect place to set up camp for the winter. There was good, clean water as well as plenty of animals to steal from the colonists. It was located at a central point on the island, making it a convenient place to defend the British position. Staying in Oyster Bay would also make it easy to dispatch his men, known as the Queen's Rangers, wherever they were needed on the Island.

Having heard that the Townsend home was the finest house in Oyster Bay, he decided that he and his men would stay there for the winter. Wasting no time upon arrival, he came straight to the house, entered through the front door, and ordered the other soldiers staying there to leave.

Sally, Phebe, and Audrey watched Colonel Simcoe from the hallway where he couldn't see them. Sally did not want to meet another British soldier. She was tired of waiting on uninvited guests and had no interest in being ordered around by another one. They watched as the Colonel introduced himself to their father.

"I will be staying here for the winter, along with a few of my officers. The rest of my men will be camped outside in the yard and around the town.

There are about three hundred of them in all." He sighed and added, "We all could use a rest."

"Have you seen a lot of fighting?" Mr. Townsend asked, eager for news of the war.

"Unfortunately, yes," the Colonel replied. "In the spring we fought in New Jersey and Pennsylvania, and during the last couple of months we fought just north of New York."

"Colonel Simcoe looks a little more refined than the others," Audrey whispered to Phebe and Sally.

Sally took another look at the large, muscular man and noticed that his face seemed friendly. But she decided not to admit this to her sisters. It didn't matter what he looked like—he was British.

"He's handsome too," Phebe agreed with Audrey. "I like all that blond, wavy hair."

"He seems too young to be a Colonel," Audrey observed. "He doesn't look much older than Robert."

They listened as the Colonel told Mr. Townsend his plans. "I will return at suppertime with my men. Have quarters ready for us by then."

The soldiers who had been living with them left quickly, leaving a mess behind. Once they were gone, Sally, Phebe, and Audrey prepared the rooms for their new guests.

When they finished, Sally went to her room to rest. But just as she lay down, she heard the sound of wood being chopped. Could the soldiers be chopping their *own* firewood for a change? Maybe the Queen's Rangers weren't so bad.

She climbed off her bed and went to the window. She looked down at the soldiers—and gasped at the horrifying scene. Under the direction of Colonel Simcoe, his men were in the orchard chopping down the trees.

"Mama!" Sally called. "Come quickly!"

Seconds later, Mrs. Townsend, followed by Audrey and Phebe, entered Sally's room. They looked out the window and were as shocked as Sally. "Samuel!" Mrs. Townsend called down to her husband. "You must stop them from chopping our trees down!" They heard the door slam as Mr. Townsend ran outside.

From the window, they watched Mr. Townsend talk to Colonel Simcoe. He gestured toward the orchard with an angry expression while the Colonel stood with his hands clasped behind his back, calmly ignoring him. Finally, Mr. Townsend returned to the house looking defeated. Mrs. Townsend and her daughters met him in the downstairs hallway.

"He said he needs the trees as a source of lumber more than we need the fruit they provide," Mr. Townsend said quietly.

"Why does he need the trees?" Sally demanded, looking out a front window. "Fruit trees hardly make

39

good lumber."

All the family members gathered at the window overlooking the orchard, watching in silence as every last fruit tree was cut down.

"All my precious apple trees," Mrs. Townsend said, sinking into a chair. "Remember, Samuel? We planted them when they were seedlings. We took care of them for years before they gave fruit."

"*Shh*, it will be all right," her husband said, putting his hands on her shoulders. "We will replant them after the war."

How can Papa be so kind? Sally wondered angrily. He was trying to comfort her mother by looking at the bright side of this ordeal. But as far as Sally was concerned, there *was* no bright side. She knew that anyone who would chop down trees that didn't belong to him was callous and mean. She refused to believe otherwise—even though she *was* a Quaker.

THAT EVENING, PHEBE, AUDREY, and Sally were in the kitchen, preparing to serve dinner to Colonel Simcoe and several of the Queen's Rangers.

"Even though they cut down the orchard they aren't as bad as the last bunch," Audrey commented.

"You're right, Audrey," Phebe agreed. "They do seem to be a bit better."

Sally shook her head in disgust. "Didn't you see how hurt Mama was while they were chopping those trees down? They make me so mad."

"This *is* war, Sally," Audrey said. "They have to do their jobs."

"I suppose so." Sally sighed. "And, it *is* quieter in the dining room. So far they've been a little more polite to us than the last soldiers. But they are still under British command, and I don't trust them."

William and David came home as the sun was getting low in the sky. They entered the kitchen, each holding a handle on either side of a basket full of oysters. The basket was dripping as they set it down. The boys, too, were wet from head to toe.

"Oysters!" said Sally. "What a treat!"

"You've almost missed dinner," Phebe scolded. "Why are you so late?"

"This might be the last day we could get oysters before the winter," David apologized. The Townsends loved eating oysters and missed them during the cold winter months.

"The water is still warm but the air is freezing," William added with a shiver.

"Shush, the soldiers will hear you," Phebe warned her brothers. "And oysters are on *our* menu—not theirs."

But the warning was too late. Colonel Simcoe, who had come to stand in the kitchen doorway, spotted the basket on the floor. "Ah, oysters," he said. "How soon will they be ready? My men would like to eat them as soon as they are cooked." Without waiting for an answer, he returned to the dining room.

"How rude!" Sally exclaimed.

"I guess we won't have any oysters until next spring," Audrey sighed. "They'll eat every last one of them—I just know it."

Phebe looked disgusted as she began to take the oysters from the basket.

"See I told you," said Sally. "They're no better than the others."

LATER, WHILE PHEBE AND SALLY were collecting the plates of empty oyster shells, Colonel Simcoe turned to Sally. "Why didn't you eat with us?" he asked.

Sally glared at him speechlessly.

"I would like your family to dine with us from now on," the Colonel continued. "I will speak to your father about the matter. I don't want you to be our servants. I don't want to disrupt your family."

Sally couldn't hold her anger in any longer. "I don't believe you," she said accusingly. "You say you don't want to disrupt our family but the truth is you probably just want to have a few girls entertain your men as they eat."

Surprised at her younger sister's outburst, Phebe gently touched Sally's arm. Sally pulled her arm away and leaned closer to the Colonel. "You just cut down our orchard," she yelled with rage. "How can you say you don't want to disrupt our family?"

She expected Colonel Simcoe to laugh at her, but he didn't. Instead he looked thoughtful. "I *am* sorry for that," he said. "But we must have a clear view in case of attack from the water. We need the trees to build fortifications on the hill across the street. This *is* a war, you know."

Sally was horrified. The Townsend home was *between* Long Island Sound and the hill. Was the Colonel planning to have a battle right in their yard? If he was, her family was certainly in harm's way.

6

A DEVELOPING FRIENDSHIP

COLONEL SIMCOE AND HIS MEN ROSE EARLY the next morning to begin building the fortifications. Sally, Mrs. Townsend, Phebe, and Audrey watched them from a window. They saw the Colonel direct his men to strip the smaller branches from the trees they had chopped down the day before, and sharpen the larger branches. After they did this, they dragged the trees to the top of the hill and stuck them in the ground, the sharp branches pointing outward to make it difficult for attackers to get in without getting hurt. Finally, they aimed a couple of small cannon from the hill toward the Sound.

"They're building an *abatis*," Audrey said, "rows of sharpened sticks. I've read about them, but this is the first time I've ever seen one."

"How can you be so calm, Audrey?" Sally asked disapprovingly. "I'm getting angrier and angrier just watching them. I'd like to get my hands on that Simcoe. Doesn't he care that our home stands between the hill and the water? If they're attacked from the water *we'll* be completely unprotected."

"Girls, girls," Mrs. Townsend murmured, though she was not really paying attention to their conversation. She was used to disagreements between Sally and her sisters though they never lasted long.

Before supper, Sally found her father in the store. "I don't want to eat in the same room with the soldiers," she said. "We're certainly not friends. I'd feel much more comfortable eating in the kitchen."

"I don't want a war in the middle of my house, too," Mr. Townsend said, looking troubled. "I believe we should all eat together."

Not wanting to cause her father any more worry, Sally agreed to eat with the rest of her family and the soldiers in the dining room—which they did from that day on.

Before the war, meals in the Townsends' dining room were fun and lively. Everyone always had something to contribute to the conversation. But now that Colonel Simcoe and his men sat with them, the Townsends were very polite and reserved. Instead, it was the Colonel and his men who carried the conversations.

For their first few weeks in Oyster Bay, the soldiers talked endlessly at suppertime about the fort they were building, dubbed "Fort Hill." When Sally looked up at the hill from the outside she saw just the sharpened trees and could only wonder what was inside. But from Colonel Simcoe's conversations with his men she gathered they built shelters for about a hundred men. The remaining soldiers camped at the foot of the hill, ready to run up to the fort if attacked. Sally noted that the Queen's Rangers kept a much more orderly camp than the previous British soldiers. Horses were kept corralled away from the living areas and garbage was regularly burned.

During the first long winter Colonel Simcoe stayed with the Townsends, Sally quietly observed how he dealt with his soldiers. When one of them had a problem, the Colonel gave him advice. When a soldier was unsure about something, the Colonel gave him instructions. And when an argument broke out among his troops, Colonel Simcoe was always there to settle it.

One evening, a neighbor of the Townsends', Mr. Blackman, burst into the dining room. "I am sorry, Samuel, for coming here like this while you are eating," he said nervously, "but I must make a complaint." He turned to face Colonel Simcoe who was wiping his mouth with a napkin. "Sir, one of your soldiers has stolen my last cow," Mr. Blackman said, twisting his hat in his hands. "My children need the milk and butter from that cow."

The Colonel put down his napkin. "Do you realize that we are in a war," he said, calmly. "and if the British army requests an item, we may have it after compensating you?"

"I understand," Mr. Blackman replied, "but nobody requested my cow and nobody paid for it. Your soldier just took it."

"Please, return to your home," the Colonel said. "I will take care of this."

"But . . . but," Mr. Blackman said.

"Please go now," Colonel Simcoe repeated sternly.

As Mr. Blackman left, Sally felt her heart reach out to him. "He's still upset," she whispered to her mother. "He'll never see the cow *or* payment."

"Sh," whispered Mrs. Townsend.

Suddenly, Colonel Simcoe stood up and barked an order to his aide. "Find out who stole that man's cow. When we need something there are rules and procedures to follow. Whoever didn't follow the rules and procedures will be punished.

"Yes, sir," the soldier said. He left his half-eaten dinner to carry out the order.

"I don't want to see any poor treatment of the townspeople," Colonel Simcoe continued after the soldier left. "We must maintain good relations with those who live here."

For a moment, Sally forgot that the Colonel was

British. His words had been warm and caring. She glanced at him and found him looking back at her. It almost seemed as if he was hoping to get her approval. *I must be imagining things,* Sally thought, looking away. Even if he'd been trying to impress her she didn't care.

When the soldier returned a short time later and announced that the cow had been returned to its owner, Sally secretly rejoiced. But when she felt the Colonel looking at her, she turned to Phebe and acted as if the news was unimportant.

From that evening on, Sally couldn't help admiring Colonel Simcoe for the fair, kind way he seemed to handle every situation. *Maybe he's not trying to impress me,* Sally thought. *Maybe he really is a decent person.* But then, she would push these thoughts aside. If she became friendly with the Colonel, then she might have to put aside her anger. And she certainly wasn't ready to do that.

As the winter drew to a close, Colonel Simcoe and his soldiers had very little to do. Neither army wanted to fight any major battles in the cold weather. During this time, Colonel Simcoe often tried to talk to Sally, but she continued to ignore him.

One day the Colonel was sitting alone in the parlor when Sally walked by. "Sally, do you know what it's like to be thousands of miles from your family?" he asked. "Do you have any idea what it's like not knowing when you will see them again?"

Sally was tempted to keep walking but his troubled manner made her stop. She thought about how terrible it would be if she were stranded in England by herself—with no Mama, Papa, brothers, or sisters. Even Robert wouldn't be there to cheer her up.

"No I don't know what it's like," Sally said, sitting down. For the first time she felt sympathy for this man. She watched him run his hand through his wavy, blond hair, and realized he was a person just like she was, with normal thoughts and feelings. No matter how hard she tried, she couldn't dislike him just because he was a British soldier.

"I have younger brothers about the same ages as David and William," the Colonel said. "I'm missing out on watching them grow up. The last letter I got from them was four months after they wrote it. I wonder what they're doing—what they're eating for supper, how their Christmas was. I hope my mother doesn't miss me too much . . . " His voice trailed off.

Sally thought about her brother Solomon. Though they received occasional letters from him during the first two years of the war, Sally missed Solomon terribly. She often wondered what he was doing and how the war was affecting him. She understood how Colonel Simcoe felt about missing his brothers.

Sally could see thinking about his family was

making him sad. "But didn't *you* decide to be a soldier?" she asked.

"Oh, yes," Colonel Simcoe said, smiling warmly. For the first time, Sally noticed how handsome he was. "I just never thought I'd be so far from my family when I became one. I attended Eton and Oxford, and could have done other things. But I'm proud of what I do. This is the most exciting profession I could imagine."

"And you're very successful at it," Sally pointed out, impressed at the mention of the two prestigious schools. "You must have been promoted when you were very young."

"Twenty-six *is* young to be a Colonel, but I was lucky," Colonel Simcoe said, modestly. "I arrived in Boston the day of the Battle of Bunker Hill. A high-ranking officer must have noticed me because, soon after the battle, I was given command of the Queen's Rangers."

Sally found herself enjoying their conversation. She admired him and decided she would try to speak to him more often. Maybe she had been too hard on him.

A FEW DAYS LATER, ROBERT CAME home for his weekly visit. Sally wondered how her brother felt about Colonel Simcoe and decided to ask him. "You've known Colonel Simcoe since he arrived here last fall," she said to him while they sat on the front porch. "But you've never told me what you think of him." There was a questioning look on her face.

Robert thought for a few seconds before replying. "I think he's very likeable. You should be nice to him," he said with a smile.

Sally didn't tell him she had already decided to be nice to the Colonel. "Why are you smiling?" she asked suspiciously. "I think you are up to something, Robert. I don't think you *really* like him. I think you want me to be nice to him for a reason. Am I right?"

"Of course I have a reason," Robert confessed.

"Tell me," Sally said.

"No, I will not," Robert teased. Then his expression became serious. "But you should try to get along with him—at least for Papa's sake. We don't want him to be arrested again."

"That's true," Sally agreed. "But it's so hard to be nice to the British," she said with a sigh. *At least most of them,* she thought.

Determined to keep her new feelings about Colonel Simcoe to herself, Sally changed the subject. "How's your business in New York?"

"How do you know about my business?" Robert demanded.

"Robert . . . your coffee shop. How is it?" Sally was puzzled by Robert's alarmed look.

"Oh, the coffee shop," Robert said, relaxing. "It's fine."

"What did you *think* I meant?"

"My *other* business," Robert said, winking. "Remind me to tell you about it some day."

Sally had suspected Robert was doing something in addition to running the coffee shop and working at Mr. Rivington's newspaper. But what could his secret be? "Robert, you're not doing something illegal like smuggling, are you?" she asked.

"Sally, Sally, Sally," Robert laughed. "I would never do anything against the law. You know that."

Sally *did* know that. She knew Robert was very honest. But she still wanted to know what her brother was up to.

"Tell me what you're hiding," she pleaded. "I want to know about it. I won't tell anyone."

"Sally, what I do is dangerous," Robert said, shaking his head. "Much too dangerous for you to know about." Then he left to help his father in the store.

A FEW WEEKS LATER, COLONEL Simcoe asked Sally for a special favor. "Would you mind having a small tea party here?" he asked. Sally was surprised to detect a note of shyness in his voice.

"I wouldn't mind at all, and I think I can say the same for my sisters," she said. There hadn't been a tea party at the Townsend home since the war began. She remembered how much fun she and her sisters used to have.

To her amazement, Sally found herself most excited about an opportunity to talk to the Colonel in her prettiest dress.

"I'll only invite a few men," the Colonel said. "They would enjoy it very much. They are far from England and they would like the company of three pretty sisters and their friends."

THE TEA PARTY TOOK PLACE on a Saturday afternoon in the early spring. Sally, Audrey, and Phebe had invited a couple of other girls from town, and Colonel Simcoe had invited a few of his officers. David and William decided a tea party was for girls and were not interested in attending.

For the first time, Sally took longer to get ready than her sisters did. When she finally did come down the stairs in a pretty, long blue velvet dress, she hoped Colonel Simcoe was watching her. She silently scolded herself for feeling nervous. After all, what was there to feel nervous about?

She searched the parlor for Colonel Simcoe and blushed when she noticed he was staring at her. He got up from his chair and walked over to her.

"You . . . you look beautiful," he said.

"Thank you," Sally said, blushing. But seeing the Colonel's own nervousness made her relax a little.

The Colonel introduced Sally to Major John André, a British officer stationed in New York. The tall officer was well-groomed, with polished buckles and a white ruffled shirt. His dark hair was pulled into a neat pony tail away from his handsome, oval face. His twinkling eyes made it look as though he were always on the brink of laughter.

While Colonel Simcoe and Major André talked, Phebe, looking pretty in a green satin dress, walked up to Sally. Sally noticed her sister gaping at the handsome Major.

"Really, Phebe," Sally whispered good-humoredly. "Do you have to stare so openly at the Major?"

Phebe blushed and looked away quickly. "I didn't realize I was staring," she said. "He's so charming. I . . . I met him a few minutes ago."

"I like him too," Sally said.

Both girls watched as Major André leaned against the mantle. He pretended to lose his balance. The girls giggled as Major André winked at them.

"He's silly too," Phebe said. "I like his sense of humor."

Colonel Simcoe walked over to Sally. "Don't be fooled by his clowning around," he said quietly. "Major André is the highest ranking aide to Commander-in-Chief Henry Clinton. He's the only person Clinton confides in about his plans."

"General Clinton is the Commander-in-Chief?" asked Sally. "Does that mean he commands all British troops?"

"All British troops in America," the Colonel replied. "He took over the position a few months after General Howe resigned at the end of 1777."

"So Major André is Clinton's right hand man," Sally said, impressed. "He seems too young to be in such a position. He can't be more than twenty-five. What is such an important person doing here?"

Major André heard Sally's question and grinned at her. "I certainly wouldn't come all this way to see this man." He put his arm around Colonel Simcoe. It was obvious the two men were close friends. "I'm here because I can't miss a party."

"It's true," Colonel Simcoe told her. "Major André goes to every party in New York and Long Island."

"Even though I *am* a soldier, I try not to let the war interfere with my social life," Major André said, laughing.

The tea party was a great success. Everyone agreed that the tiny cakes Audrey and Phebe had made the day before were delicious. Though Sally spent a lot of time talking to Major André and Colonel Simcoe, she made sure to talk to all the guests. After all, she was one of the hostesses.

"Most of the men in the Queen's Rangers are British colonists who are loyal to the crown," said a British officer whom Sally was conversing with at the moment. He was trying to explain to her the origin of the regiment.

"Oh, really?" she said, barely hearing him. She was much too busy watching Colonel Simcoe across the room. His familiar smile was so gentle and kind. Why had it taken her so long to notice it? And why was he talking so much to Phebe's friend Charlotte? She hoped the Colonel didn't find Charlotte too pretty.

When the soldier Sally had been talking with went to refill his teacup, the Colonel excused himself from his conversation and joined Sally. She was relieved and thrilled that he stayed by her side for the rest of the party. *What a thoroughly enjoyable day*, she thought. The tea party had been such a success that they had another one a week later. Soon tea parties at the Townsend home became a regular event.

7

A VALENTINE

BY THE FALL OF 1779, SALLY'S FRIENDSHIP with Colonel Simcoe had grown even warmer. The Colonel and the Queen's Rangers had been living with the Townsend's for almost a year. Since there had been no battles in the North that winter or spring, they spent almost all their time in Oyster Bay.

Things, however, were very grim for the patriots. Robert kept the Townsends updated on the latest news. British General Henry Clinton had left New York with his troops, heading south. He knew there were plenty of Southern colonists loyal to the King. He was also aware that Washington's army got much of their food and financial support from the South. If General Clinton could take the southern colonies, then he could cut Washington's supply lines.

One morning, Colonel Simcoe was in the parlor reading *The Royal Gazette*. When one of his soldiers entered the room and whispered in his ear, he put down the paper. "Mrs. Townsend, can you come here for a moment?" he called.

Sally, curious about what business the Colonel had with her mother, followed her downstairs.

"Come outside, Mrs. Townsend," Colonel Simcoe said warmly, winking at Sally. Then he took Mrs. Townsend by the hand and led her out to the porch. On the street they saw a cart full of sticks, some with a few leaves on them.

"What are they, Colonel?" Sally asked.

"They're trees," Colonel Simcoe said proudly. "Apple and pear trees. My men will plant them for you over there." He pointed toward an area a short distance from the house.

Speechless, Mrs. Townsend walked around the cart, touching the leaves and branches. "Oh, Colonel," was all she could manage to say. She was beaming.

"I must apologize for cutting down your orchard," the Colonel said, "though it was my duty and responsibility to do it. I'm truly sorry, and I hope this will only begin to make up for it."

"Colonel Simcoe, you are too kind," Mrs. Townsend said. "You did not have to do this. It must have been very hard for you to get the trees."

The Colonel shrugged it off, gazing at Sally. Sally was used to his special looks by now and did not turn away. Several months earlier, she considered all the colonists to be fine, upstanding people while all British were evil. Now she knew there were kind and honorable men on both sides.

Everything was becoming so confusing. She sided with the Rebels because their fight was for freedom from an unjust government. But she also couldn't help feeling sympathy for the British because of the way she felt about Colonel Simcoe.

Sally's relationship with Colonel Simcoe was beginning to change. When she wasn't with the Colonel, she was always thinking about him. And soon she found herself wanting to be with him all the time.

AS THE LEAVES CHANGED COLOR and then fell off the trees, Sally's affection for Colonel Simcoe continued to deepen. One winter day, Robert came home for his weekly visit. He and Sally put on warm clothing and went for a walk in the snow. They ended up sitting quietly on a log, gazing out over Oyster Bay. Though it was cold outside, Sally welcomed the quiet and stillness. As she looked out over the water she thought about Hannah, as she so often had over the past three years. Sally had given up expecting her to return—at least not until after the war. Would Hannah still be the same as she always was? Did Hannah have a new best friend? What if Hannah was married? It was possible. She would be eighteen now, old enough to be someone's wife. Then, she'd never come back . . .

"Here, I think you dropped this," Robert said, pulling Sally away from her thoughts. He handed her a folded piece of paper.

When Sally unfolded the paper and read her own crooked handwriting she wanted to die from embarrassment. "Robert, please tell me nobody else saw this," Sally pleaded. *"Mrs. Simcoe . . . Mrs. John Graves Simcoe . . . Sally Simcoe."* Earlier that day Sally had been practicing writing what her new name would be if she married the Colonel. She never expected anyone else to see it.

"Nobody else saw it," Robert said, amused. "Your secret is safe with me. But I thought you were disgusted by the British." He reached over and playfully tugged on her hair. "Why, I even heard you call them *animals* at one time. Now you're considering marrying one of them?"

"Stop, Robert." Sally felt herself blushing. "I care for Colonel Simcoe very much."

"I've noticed," Robert said. "Everybody has. You stare at each other all the time."

"You don't think he's too old for me, do you?" Sally asked. "He's about your age."

Robert smiled. "He's not too old."

"So, Robert, you don't care that he is British?" Sally asked, relieved to have someone to talk to.

"What can I do?" Robert said, shrugging. "I can't say I like it. In fact, I don't like the British at all. I only hope that if you hear anything from him you'll let me know."

"What do you mean?" Sally asked. "You act as if you're a spy or something."

"Shhh!" Robert said in a low voice grabbing Sally's arm. He looked around to make sure no one heard him. "Sally, you could get me killed with talk like that."

"Well, that's how you've been acting, Robert." Sally waited for her brother to confess whatever he had been hiding.

"Sally, it's very complicated . . ." Robert began, "but, if you overhear anything important . . . I know how to reach Washington."

"*General* Washington?" Sally gasped. "Robert, what you are doing is very, very dangerous. Remember Nathan Hale? You're the one who told me about him. How many others have the British hanged since? They wouldn't think twice about putting a rope around your neck and hanging you until your face turned blue and you were dead."

"Sally, I'm not a spy!" Robert said, grinning at his sister's imagination. "I just want you to tell me if you hear any information from your Colonel."

"I'll tell you," Sally promised.

Later that day, however, she wondered what

would happen to Colonel Simcoe if she told Robert something she had heard him or another British officer say. If she were to find out where Simcoe and the Queen's Rangers were going next and told Robert, couldn't Colonel Simcoe and his men get killed? She shuddered at the thought of sending her Colonel to his death. She hoped the situation would never come up.

ON THE MORNING OF VALENTINE'S Day, the Townsend sisters were preparing for one of their weekly tea parties. Phebe and Audrey had dressed early and were downstairs helping prepare refreshments while Sally was still in her room dressing. As she combed her hair, she noticed a piece of paper that had been slipped under the door. She picked it up, unfolded it, and felt her heart pound. It was a valentine from Colonel Simcoe! Sally felt her face flush as she read:

Fairest Maid! Where all are fair,
Beauty's pride and Nature's care;
To you my heart I must resign,
O choose me for your Valentine!

Sally's eyes filled with tears. She couldn't even finish reading the rest of the poem. Colonel Simcoe thought she was the fairest! *I do choose you for my*

Valentine, Colonel John Graves Simcoe! she thought proudly.

Sally hurried down the stairs, searching for the Colonel. For the first time she was completely certain that she was in love with Colonel Simcoe and couldn't wait to be with him. She saw him beaming up at her from the bottom of the stairs.

"Did you get what I left under your door?" the Colonel whispered.

"Yes," Sally said softly, holding his gaze with her eyes.

"Yes what?" he asked.

"Yes, I'll be your Valentine," Sally said warmly.

Just then, Major André, who planned to stay for a couple of days, arrived. Everybody was happy to see him. He amused Audrey, Phebe, and several others with his jokes all evening. Sally and Colonel Simcoe, however, were much too preoccupied with each other to be entertained by anybody else.

Sally knew she had never felt so happy in her life. Every few minutes, she felt for the valentine in her pocket—just to make sure it was real. She wondered how she could ever have disliked Colonel Simcoe, a man she now thought to be the most wonderful in the world. Neither of them left the other's side for the entire evening.

8

THE BATTLE

AFTER THE TEA PARTY, AUDREY AND PHEBE were thrilled when Sally showed them Colonel Simcoe's valentine.

"How romantic!" said Phebe. "I want to meet someone as handsome as he is."

"I do too, Phebe," Audrey said.

"But Phebe," Sally teased, "I thought you told me after the last tea party that Major André was the most handsome man you ever met."

"Well they're both handsome," Phebe said diplomatically. "Maybe Major André will write a valentine for *me* next year." she added hopefully.

Sally showed the Valentine to her mother in the parlor the following morning. "He wrote this himself . . . for me," Sally said, beaming. "I can't stop daydreaming about him."

"It's very nice, dear," Mrs. Townsend said, putting her arm around Sally's shoulder. "He seems to care about you very much."

Suddenly Sally felt troubled. "Mama, it's not that I like the British," she said, "because I don't."

"Sally, dear, we try to like everyone," said Mrs. Townsend.

"Yes, but I detest British policy toward the colonies," said Sally. "And I don't like the way the soldiers treat the Colonists."

"A young lady shouldn't involve herself in politics," her mother said.

"But, Mama," Sally persisted. "What if I were faced with a decision? What if I had to choose between doing what I thought was right for the Colonists and how I feel for Colonel Simcoe."

Mrs. Townsend looked into her daughter's eyes, realizing that her daughter was serious about wanting to find an honorable answer. "Sally," she said, "Do you know the saying, 'love the sinner but hate the sin'?"

"What do you mean?" Sally asked.

"Well, you know that as Quakers, we do not believe in war nor do we take sides," Mrs. Townsend began. "We care for people no matter which side they're on—even if we don't approve of their actions. Most of us don't like what the participants of this war are doing to each other, but that doesn't stop us from believing there are good individuals on both sides."

"And how does this help how I feel about the Colonel?" Sally asked.

"I can see that you care about *him*," said Mrs. Townsend, "but you don't care for what he and his troops are doing. I understand how you feel and, in a way, I feel the same."

"What if I have to make a decision?" Sally asked.

Mrs. Townsend hugged her daughter close. "You are nearly a grown woman, Sally," she said. "If, some day, you feel as though you must make a decision, then I suggest you pay attention to the actions of each side. Favor the side whose actions represent freedom and justice, what is right and what is good."

"Thank you, Mama," Sally said, hugging her mother. "You've helped me. I just hope I never have to choose."

"I do too, dear." Mrs. Townsend smiled.

DURING THE WAR, WASHINGTON'S men often came over at night from Connecticut to raid the British. They would cross Long Island Sound in small whaleboats to steal British supplies and arms, and to destroy whatever the British held. Sometimes the raiders weren't even fighting for independence—they were merely pirates who stole from everyone, British and Colonists alike.

One night when everyone was asleep, Sally was awakened by the sound of gunfire. In her long white nightgown, she ran out into the hallway while her sisters stayed in bed, too afraid to move. Soldiers were everywhere—rushing out of rooms, gathering up gear, and quickly running out of the house.

In all the confusion, Sally made her way to the stairs and bumped—*smack*—into a soldier who was trying to run back up the stairs. It was Colonel Simcoe!

"Sally . . . Sally, there you are," he said with relief. He took both her hands in his. "We're under attack. Keep your head down. Don't look out the windows. As he ran down the stairs, he called back to her. "Stay down. I'll be back."

Terrified, Sally ran back to the room she shared with Phebe and Audrey. Her sisters were both in Phebe's bed with their arms around each other. Their fearful expressions were exaggerated in the flickering candlelight. Every few seconds, an exploding cannon lit up the room from outside. Over the noise of the gunfire, Sally yelled Colonel Simcoe's instructions to Audrey and Phebe. The two of them crept out of bed and crouched onto the floor next to Sally.

Though Sally was scared, the excitement thrilled her. Despite her fears, she couldn't resist looking out the window.

"Get away from the window!" Phebe cried. "Sally, get over here." Sally pretended she couldn't hear her sister.

With each flash of the cannon, Sally caught glimpses of men running in every direction. Everything seemed to be in a state of confusion. She searched for Colonel Simcoe but couldn't find him. She could, however, see the attackers racing away in the direction of the shore. Hearing the sound of a musket ball hitting the side of the house, she quickly crouched down again with her panicked sisters.

Phebe was crying.

"Don't worry," Sally said as she put her arm around her sister. "It will be over soon. Now that the Rebels have attacked, they're running back to their boats as quickly as they can.

"I hope you're right," said Audrey.

Sally wondered if Colonel Simcoe was all right. She hadn't seen him outside. Then she was struck by a terrible thought. What if the Colonel had been shot? The idea sickened her, causing the excitement to disappear. Her first instinct was to run out of the house to look for him, but she resisted the temptation.

Finally, the sounds of gunfire began to fade. Phebe's sobs became whimpers. "I thought it would never end," whispered Audrey.

By now, the British soldiers were shouting loudly to each other in the yard. The girls got up to look out the window just as Mr. and Mrs. Townsend entered their room. William and David joined them a few moments later.

"Thank God you're all right," Mrs. Townsend cried, hugging all three of her daughters.

Thank God you and Papa were not hurt," Sally replied.

There was a knock on the open bedroom door. "Is everyone all right?"

Sally felt her heart beat faster as she recognized Colonel Simcoe's voice. She was so happy, she had to restrain herself from running over to him.

"We're all fine," said Mr. Townsend. "How are your men? Is anyone injured?"

"We had a couple of flesh wounds that are being attended to now," the Colonel said, looking over Mr. Townsend's shoulder. His eyes rested when they met Sally's eyes. His worried expression relaxed into a relieved smile at seeing her unharmed.

"Can you use our help?" Mrs. Townsend asked.

"I think we can, Mrs. Townsend," the Colonel said gratefully. "Please help tend to the wounded men." He took one last look at Sally before turning and accompanying Mrs. Townsend down the stairs.

Sally felt herself tremble—partly from the excitement of the battle but also from her feelings for the Colonel. She was certain of one thing: she cared much more deeply for Colonel Simcoe than she had thought. She had been ready to run out in the middle of the battle to risk her life for him.

9

IMPORTANT INFORMATION

EVER SINCE SALLY TOLD HER MOTHER ABOUT the valentine, Mrs. Townsend had made it a point to get better acquainted with Colonel Simcoe. The better she got to know him, the more pleased she was with his affection for her daughter. "It makes me happy that everyone gets along so well," she said to Sally one afternoon as they sat sewing in the parlor. "And I'm especially pleased about you and the Colonel."

"Even though he's British?" Sally asked.

"Even though he's British," Mrs. Townsend said. "Now we just have to find good men for Phebe and Audrey."

Sally thought about Major André and hoped he had some affection for Phebe.

"Come and help me pack some baskets of food," said Mrs. Townsend.

Sally didn't have to ask what the baskets were for.

Her mother was always sending baskets of food or clothing to people in need. She seemed to be concerned about everyone in Oyster Bay. Sally put down her sewing and followed her mother outside to the smokehouse to get some turkey and deer meat.

"The British took away almost everything the Coopers owned," Mrs. Townsend said. "Hopefully this food will hold them over until they get more supplies."

"It wasn't one of the Queen's Rangers who took everything, was it?" Sally asked quickly.

"No," said Mrs. Townsend. "Otherwise I would have asked the Colonel to take care of the situation."

When they came back from the smokehouse and entered the kitchen, Sally and Mrs. Townsend heard loud laughter near the front door. They hurried to see what was happening. Major André, who had become a frequent visitor, was pointing to a window. "Now, isn't this sweet?" he said. Sally saw that etched in a pane of glass were the words: *Sally, the adorable miss.*

She felt her face flush with embarrassment, though she was thrilled. She knew the Colonel had done it. Her heart was bursting with joy. Was this what it felt like to be in love?

"Where is the Colonel?" Major André asked, winking. "I must have a word with him about this." He strode off, laughing, in search of his friend.

"Oh, Mama, isn't the Colonel wonderful?" Sally said dreamily.

THE LAST DAYS OF 1779 PASSED quickly. That winter was the coldest anyone could remember. All the water surrounding Manhattan Island was frozen solid, including the Hudson River and New York Harbor. Much of Long Island Sound was frozen too, allowing people to cross from Connecticut to Long Island on foot, sometimes a distance of twenty miles. The snow on the ground lay several feet thick. Everyone, including Colonel Simcoe and his Rangers spent much of their time indoors, trying to stay warm. Most of the major fighting was now taking place in the Carolinas and Virginia.

Ever since Sally and the Colonel became close friends, things had become peaceful. By now, she and her sisters were happy to cook for the British soldiers. And Colonel Simcoe made sure the Townsends had every comfort available to them. He insisted that his soldiers did their part in chopping firewood and carrying water from the well.

Every morning Sally woke early and dressed quickly, looking forward to seeing the Colonel at the breakfast table. But she enjoyed evenings the most when the Townsends, the Colonel, and a few of the Queen's Rangers sat in the parlor playing cards, reading aloud to each other, and having lively conversations. Rather than being a divided household, they were like one large, extended family.

The only time Sally was unhappy was when Colonel Simcoe was away. Periodically he would meet fellow officers in New York or go on hunting trips to other parts of Long Island. Despite her numerous chores, Sally found these days to be long and boring.

As spring turned into summer, Sally became more and more impatient for the war to end. She was certain that the Colonel was planning to ask for her hand in marriage after the war was over. He hinted about it every so often. He had even mentioned introducing Sally to his family. Sally couldn't wait to say yes to him. She looked forward to beginning their life together.

During that summer of 1780, Colonel Simcoe often told Sally he thought the war was almost over. He felt sure Washington's army was on the verge of collapse. Robert, however, had a different opinion. He told Sally that even though the patriots were not in great shape, they were expecting more French troops to arrive in Newport, Rhode Island, to reinforce Washington's army.

One day toward the end of the summer, Sally, Phebe, and Audrey watched from a window as Colonel Simcoe drilled his men in the heat. Major André stood next to the Colonel as the soldiers marched in the hot sun. The two men had just returned from a month-long hunting trip with General Clinton, miles away in East Hampton.

"Do we have any cakes left over from this morning?" Audrey asked.

"I hope so," said Phebe. "Life always turns into a party when Major André comes around."

"Why, Phebe, I do believe you are *still* interested in Major André," Sally teased.

"So what if I am?" Phebe replied. "It's always fun when he's here . . . and I think Audrey has a little crush on him too."

"Me?" Audrey asked with a smile. They all laughed and rushed down to the kitchen to prepare a tray of food. The girls were still in the kitchen when they heard Colonel Simcoe and Major André come into the cool shade of the parlor. "What a hot summer it has been," they heard the Colonel say. "There isn't even a mild breeze blowing across the Sound."

"You should try New York," André said. "It's so hot there it's hard to breathe."

"How is our friend coming along?" the Colonel asked. "Is he ready to see our side of things?"

After a few seconds of silence, Colonel Simcoe said, "You may speak freely. The only ones here are the young ladies in the kitchen and they don't involve themselves with politics."

Phebe had been about to carry the tray out to

the two men when Sally pulled her back. "Sssh, Phebe," she whispered, her finger to her lips. "Wait a minute. I want to hear what they're saying."

"So what have we promised our dear Benedict Arnold?" Colonel Simcoe asked Major André.

"In return for handing over the Rebel fort at West Point to our side, he will receive 20,000 pounds and a very nice command with the British army."

"That's quite a sum of money," Colonel Simcoe commented. "That should keep him well appointed for the rest of his life."

"*And* his wife," André added humorously.

"What's she like?"

"She's tiny with blond hair and blue eyes, and very, very charming," Major André said. "Though she's only nineteen, she can change the General's mind. He'd do anything for his little wife."

"This could be the turning point of the war," Colonel Simcoe said. "As soon as we have control over West Point, we can sail up the Hudson River and take the rebel strongholds one by one."

"That's right," André said. "And once we have control of the river the colonies will be divided. There won't be any way for the Rebels in Connecticut, Massachusetts, or Rhode Island to get to New York, New Jersey, or points further to the south."

"Ah, it would be so nice to end this war and go

home," Colonel Simcoe said with a sigh.

"Let's go in now," Sally whispered, letting go of Phebe's arm.

The two men smiled when Sally and Phebe entered the parlor.

"There you are," Sally said, pretending she hadn't heard a thing. "We've been busy squeezing lemons for your lemonade."

"My dear Sally," Colonel Simcoe said. "These refreshments are very much appreciated. We've been working hard outside in the heat."

"We know," Phebe said.

"We've been watching you sit in the shade ordering your men to march in the sun," Sally added. The Colonel laughed, enjoying a playful tease.

For the first time in a while, Sally wasn't in the mood to talk to the Colonel, nor to laugh at Major André's jokes. But the two men talked on and on. *Phebe and Audrey must not realize the importance of what we overheard,* Sally thought, watching her sisters enjoy themselves. Sally acted just as warm and friendly as she always had, but her mind was racing. She remembered Robert saying, "If you ever hear any information . . ." She just had to let him know what she had just heard.

After what seemed like ages, the men finished their lemonade and the girls offered to make some more.

"Did you hear what they were talking about before?" Sally whispered when the three girls reached the kitchen.

"No, I didn't," Phebe said. "Something about the war. I can't stand to hear about it anymore so I never really pay attention."

Sally rolled her eyes. "Tell them I went to a neighbor's house to borrow some sugar," she whispered. "I'll be back in a few minutes."

"But Sally, we *have* plenty of sugar," Audrey said, looking confused.

"Whatever you do, don't tell *them* that," Sally said. "Trust me. This is important. Tell them what I told you and do *not* tell them we have plenty of sugar."

Phebe and Audrey nodded their heads gravely realizing how serious their sister was.

Sally hurried down the road to the tavern and went inside. It didn't take long to find someone she could hire to go to New York to give Robert a message. The tavern owner's son said he'd do it.

"Tell him his sister Sally needs him to come home at once," she said. After giving him the address of the coffee shop Robert worked in, she rushed back home and was relieved to find Phebe and Audrey just putting the lemonade on the tray. She hadn't been missed at all.

THAT EVENING, WHILE THEY WERE eating supper, Robert appeared—unexpectedly to everyone except Sally. She hoped Colonel Simcoe and his men weren't suspicious about Robert's coming home on a Tuesday rather than a Sunday, but they didn't seem to notice anything odd. They were too busy enjoying the food and conversation.

Whenever Colonel Simcoe smiled at her, Sally smiled back nervously, feeling guilty about her earlier deception.

She watched Robert put his hands on his mother's shoulders and bend down to kiss her cheek. "I missed Mama and was wishing for some of her good, home-cooked food," he said grinning.

"Really, Robert, did you come home to see me or to eat?" Mrs. Townsend asked, pleased that her son was home nonetheless.

"Why, to see you of course," said Robert, "but please give me a plate—quick." Then his eyes met Sally's. She knew he must have jumped on a horse as soon as he'd gotten her message.

Robert ate as if he were starving. Sally also ate quickly but thought it cautious to stay at the table until everyone else was finished. After convincing Phebe and Audrey to clean up without her, she slipped out the back door and away from the house. Robert joined her a few minutes later and, in silence, they walked toward the harbor in the cool darkness.

"So, Sister," Robert said after a few minutes. "I guess you heard some important information."

"I really *did* hear something," Sally said. "I think one of Washington's generals, Arnold Benedict—"

"Benedict Arnold," Robert corrected her.

"Well, I think he's going to turn the fort at West Point over to the British," Sally said. She quickly told him everything she knew.

"I believe it," said Robert, looking thoughtful. "Benedict Arnold is not very well liked. He was passed over for promotions. He was even reprimanded by General Washington once. You did the right thing by making sure I got this information, Sally. You don't realize how important it is."

"I think I do," Sally said. "I heard Colonel Simcoe and Major André talking about how this could be the turning point of the war." She stopped and stared back at the lighted windows of the house.

"I'm going to leave as soon as I can without arousing their suspicions," said Robert.

THAT NIGHT SALLY TOSSED AND turned, unable to fall asleep. She was afraid for Robert. She wondered what would become of General Arnold now that his secret was out. There were lots of questions she wanted to ask Robert the next morning. Though she rose early, Robert had already left, back to New York to see that the secret message was forwarded to General Washington.

10

SAVING WEST POINT

SALLY DIDN'T HEAR A THING ABOUT WEST Point or Benedict Arnold for quite a while. Robert hadn't been home in weeks and she and her family were starting to worry. Then one day in the middle of October, Robert came home again. Sally could tell by his face that he was deeply troubled.

"Sorry, Robert, we're all out of home-cooked food today," she said, trying to cheer him up. "You'll have to come back another day."

Robert stared at the floor. When Mrs. Townsend asked if he felt sick, he said he was fine. His mother knew better than to keep asking.

Sally waited impatiently for an opportunity to talk to Robert alone. Finally, after supper, Robert glanced at her and then left the house, saying he was going for a walk.

"Do you mind if I go with you?" Sally asked quickly. "I could use some fresh air too."

"No, Sally, I don't mind," Robert said solemnly. "Come along." Sally promised Phebe and Audrey that she'd wash the dishes herself the next night, and left the house.

As soon as they were alone, Sally took Robert's hand and tried to pass under his arm as if they were dancing. Robert smiled slightly before his grim expression returned. Sally knew her brother had something to tell her.

"You were absolutely right about West Point and the plot to surrender it to the British," Robert said.

"Really?" Sally asked. "So I must have heard everything correctly then."

"Yes," said Robert. "It seems that General Arnold's wife is very cunning. She went to one of the patriot leaders and asked him to appoint her husband to the post at West Point. We found out about it just in time to stop their plan."

"You did?" Sally asked, relieved. Robert nodded. "Have you heard anything about Major André?" she asked. "We haven't seen him in weeks."

"I have some very bad news for you, Sally," Robert said, stopping to face her. He paused. It seemed as if he was having trouble finding the right words. Finally he started speaking again. "Washington's men caught Major André after he met with Benedict Arnold. He tried to escape, dressed as a civilian by the name of John Anderson, but he was captured and held as a spy."

"Oh, no!" Sally was horrified. "Is he in prison?"

"No, I'm afraid he was hanged."

Suddenly, Sally's mind was swimming with thoughts. She remembered how much fun she and her sisters always had when Major André was around. He had an unforgettable sense of humor. *Colonel Simcoe will be devastated when he hears,* she thought. Major André had been one of his closest friends. Now he was dead. Was it all because of her? She shivered as Robert talked on.

"Everyone liked him—even his guards. Tears were rolling down their faces as they hanged him." Robert gently placed his hands on Sally's shoulders and looked her in the eye. "Sally, I know what you're thinking," he said. "But if you hadn't told me what you knew, many of our own men would have died."

Though she understood this to be true, Sally still felt miserable. She nodded to show her appreciation for her brother's words.

"You were very brave, Sally," Robert continued. "You put yourself at risk to help our country. If the British knew it was you who gave me the information about Benedict Arnold, you might have been hanged instead. You helped the war effort, and hopefully, if we win this war, the British will never mistreat us again."

By now, tears were running down Sally's face.

"Really . . . you did the right thing . . . "

Even though she felt awful, Sally forced herself to think about what could have happened if she hadn't told Robert what she had heard. For one thing, she and her family would always be living under unjust and unfair British rulers.

"Do *you* feel bad about Major André?" Sally asked Robert.

Robert nodded. "He was one of the few British soldiers that I liked. But if I had been caught passing information to Washington, then I would have been hanged. I still might be," he added, thoughtfully.

"What? What are you talking about?" Sally asked. "Isn't it all over? Didn't they stop General Arnold from turning the fort over to the British?"

"No, it's not over," said Robert. "We have a whole network of people who listen for information and pass it along until it reaches Washington. Benedict Arnold went over to the British side before we could capture him. Now he's in New York and he's furious. He wants to find out who betrayed him. If he ever comes up with any names, I . . . I don't want to think about what would happen."

"Oh, no!" Sally exclaimed.

"Some of those people are my friends," said Robert. "I told the ones in New York to leave town. All we can do now is wait to see what happens. Arnold is having people pulled off the streets and arrested, but, so far, he can't prove anything against them."

"Why can't he prove anything?" Sally asked. "Doesn't he know any names?"

"We used numbers instead of names to be safe," Robert explained. "Each person involved in passing information was assigned a number so our identities would be kept secret. Even General Washington doesn't know our real names. My code name is Culper, Jr.," Robert whispered, looking over his shoulder.

"How clever," Sally said, pleased that Robert was finally confiding in her about his spying operation. Before, he had only hinted about what he had been doing in New York. "You *never* used real names? And where did you gather your information?" Sally asked.

"The coffee shop," Robert answered. "It was always full of British soldiers. I pretended to be doing research for my newspaper articles. Then I would write a letter to a friend about everyday things. Then, in between the lines, I would write the secret information I collected in invisible ink. Washington has a chemical that makes invisible ink reappear. So, if the letter were ever found by the British, it would appear to be just an ordinary letter."

"How did you get your letters to General Washington?" Sally asked.

"It wasn't easy," Robert said, "especially since I

was usually surrounded by the British. But I always managed to work it out. A tavern owner from Setauket would come to New York under the pretense of needing supplies for his business. While he was in the city he'd pick up the letter."

"He came all the way from Setauket?" Sally asked, surprised. "That's out on the eastern end of Long Island, over fifty miles from the city."

"I know," said Robert. "But we had to use a very roundabout way to get the letters out. A crew of Washington's men would row to Setauket from Connecticut to pick them up. Then they were hand-delivered to Washington."

Suddenly Robert paused. "Listen, Sally," he said, looking grave. "This could be dangerous for you, too. I'm absolutely serious. If I'm arrested, Colonel Simcoe will know it was you who passed the information on to me, which means he'll know that you're the person who caused his friend's death. If I'm arrested, you must flee. Pay someone to contact one of the whaleboat raiders to bring you over to Connecticut. Then you can go stay with Mama's relatives in Rode Island. Do you understand me?"

Sally nodded. She wanted to tell her brother that Colonel Simcoe would never have her arrested but she remained quiet.

"I came home to tell you about this, Sally," Robert said gently. "I have a friend in the city. If I'm arrested, he'll ride out here as fast as possible to warn you. Then, you must go immediately. You *must* escape if they get me," he said forcefully.

Sally couldn't think about escaping. She was much too worried about Robert now.

"I don't feel like walking anymore," Robert said. "Let's get back to the house. I'd like to spend some time with Mama and Papa before I leave. I don't have to rush back because I've closed the coffee shop down for a couple of weeks."

Sally didn't feel like walking either, but she wasn't looking forward to returning home. She was too afraid Colonel Simcoe would notice her mood and ask what was wrong. She wondered when he'd find out about Major André. Part of her wanted to be there to comfort him when he found out. The other part of her wanted to be miles away.

When they reached the house, Sally put all thoughts of death and danger in the back of her mind. Then she forced a smile as bright as she could manage.

Her smile quickly faded when she spotted Phebe sitting in the parlor sobbing. Her mother and Audrey were trying to comfort her, with tears in their eyes as well. Colonel Simcoe sat slumped in a chair wearing a dark expression. Sally felt a wave of nausea, realizing they had all learned about Major André. When Audrey told her the news, she didn't have to pretend. Instead she burst into genuine tears. *So this is what war is about?*, she thought bitterly. *Fighting for a cause even if people you cared for died because of it?* Sally was horrified that she had played a part in it.

"Come here, Sally," the Colonel said, reaching out his hand.

Sally knew he wanted to comfort her, but she couldn't look him in the eye. Instead, she ran from the parlor and hurried up the stairs to her room. Still crying, she took the Colonel's valentine out of her top drawer and read it again for the thousandth time. This time a tear fell on it. Was she ever going to be able to face Colonel Simcoe now that everything had changed? Would things ever go back to normal? Sally stayed in her room for the rest of the evening.

THE FOLLOWING MORNING SHE didn't go downstairs to breakfast, hoping to avoid the Colonel.

After breakfast, Phebe came in carrying a tray. "Sally, Colonel Simcoe wants you to know he's leaving for battle later today," she said. Her eyes were red and swollen from crying.

Sally shrugged as if she didn't care.

"What's the matter with you?" Phebe scolded. "He really wants to say goodbye to you."

Sally sighed, knowing that as difficult as it might

be, she'd have to face him. She went downstairs to find the Colonel standing in the front hallway ready to leave. "Good-bye and good luck to you," she said quickly, unable to meet the Colonel's eyes. "Come back safely." But as much as she loved him, she wasn't sure she could ever face him again.

"Sally!" Colonel Simcoe exclaimed, taking her in his arms. "It pains me to have to leave you at a time like this. I know you and your family are very upset by what has happened."

Sally felt a lump in her throat as her eyes filled with tears. She felt so warm and safe in the Colonel's embrace that part of her wanted to stay in his arms forever. Yet another part of her knew she had betrayed him.

"I feel just as devastated as you do," said the Colonel. "The other side knew of our plan ahead of time." Suddenly, the Colonel's tone changed to one Sally hadn't heard before. "If I ever find out who was behind this, I'll kill him with my bare hands. I owe that much to my dear friend André."

Sally felt her body stiffen in fear. Hoping the Colonel wouldn't notice this, she slipped out of his embrace. The furious look on his face made her shudder. She was no longer confident that the Colonel would never hurt her or have her arrested. His unfamiliar tone and expression scared her into believing he would probably kill her if he ever found out the truth.

At that moment, Sally knew that no matter what it took, she'd have to find a way to get over her love for Colonel Simcoe. They could never spend their lives together with this dreadful secret between them.

During the weeks following Colonel Simcoe's departure from the Townsend's, Sally waited nervously for word from Robert. Though she dreaded having to leave home, she was always ready to run if she had to.

As time went on with no urgent messages from Robert, Sally began to feel that she was no longer in danger. Eventually things went back to normal— that is, everything except for Sally and Colonel Simcoe's relationship. When the Colonel returned, Sally found that her secret kept her from becoming any closer to him.

In the winter after Benedict Arnold went over to the British side, he became Colonel Simcoe's commanding officer. He and General Arnold went to Sandy Hook, New Jersey, and from there headed for Virginia. As the war raged on in the South, General Arnold and Colonel Simcoe fought in battles throughout Virginia. At first, Sally missed having the Colonel around, but eventually she became accustomed to his long absences.

The war finally ended two years after Sally had passed Robert the information about Arnold. In November of 1782, provisional treaties were signed. Then the following year, a definitive treaty was signed, recognizing the colonies' independence from Britain.

After the war, Colonel Simcoe remained in the British army but was stationed in Canada. He never found out that Sally had been the "spy" who had saved West Point and caused the death of his friend. He went on to have an illustrious career serving his majesty. He died as a viceroy in India.

Soon after the war had ended, Robert came home again to run the family business. Although all their brothers and sisters left home to start families, Sally and Robert remained in Oyster Bay and never married. Sally lived a happy life, though. Every so often, she'd take out her valentine and dream about how her life might have been if things had turned out differently.